FRAGMENTS

FRAGMENTS

BECOMING WHO WE ARE

DEBORAH BALLARD

TATE PUBLISHING
AND ENTERPRISES, LLC

Published by Tate Publishing & Enterprises, LLC
127 E. Trade Center Terrace | Mustang, Oklahoma 73064 USA
1.888.361.9473 | www.tatepublishing.com

Tate Publishing is committed to excellence in the publishing industry. The company reflects the philosophy established by the founders, based on Psalm 68:11,
"The Lord gave the word and great was the company of those who published it."

Book design copyright © 2015 by Tate Publishing, LLC. All rights reserved.
Cover design by Samson Lim
Interior design by Jomel Pepito

Published in the United States of America

ISBN: 978-1-68118-173-8
1. Fiction / Action & Adventure
2. Fiction / Short Stories (Single Author)
15.05.19

Fragments is the fictional story of three young women's lives who rose from obscure backgrounds to becoming three of the most influential women of God of all time. Their lives, their journeys, their calls. Each one different and unique and each one equally valued and loved by a loving God. This book will have you captivated as we explore the very reaches of the human heart and its ultimate call…to love.

It was 3:00 a.m. As I lay awake, in the hope of sleep, the rustling of the gum tree leaves on the big ghost gum outside my bedroom window had me mesmerized. The full moon made the gum tree glow, which added to my fixation with its form and mysterious presence in the night time scene.

At fifteen, I longed for an extraordinary life. A life filled with adventure, risk, and meaning. I dreamt of great journeys to far-reaching lands where the helpless and forgotten were in need of heroes and heroines to save their souls from isolating loneliness and the dangers of these hidden worlds that were sometimes life-threatening and unpredictable. Lives that needed someone to care enough that they lived a better life, a life full of hope and trust, not fear and doubt.

I had heard of the missionaries. I learned about some of their lives in youth church on Friday nights. "Call of God," the youth leaders said. Once God had put the fire in their hearts to go on mission, nothing would stop the fire burning in their hearts to go and save souls from circumstances that sometimes would threaten even the missionaries' lives. Trust and faith led them; God protected them.

I imagined myself in the depths of the deep, dense rainforest areas in the hinterlands of the Nile River, a somewhat romantic notion and a typical missionary imagining. This was only a very small part of what God had planned for my life when I was to turn twenty-two. What we imagine as the road ahead very rarely ends up being the whole plan that God intends for our lives. Seven more years and I would be on the adventure of my life…and also running for my life!

My life at home was less than perfect. Three brothers and two older sisters had Mum scrambling to meet our needs. Mum did what she could. With only two arms, two legs, and a faith in God that no man could shake, she managed to pull us all through school and on to jobs or further study. Mum was one of my greatest heroines. She continued to amaze me with how she got things done. Sure, we would all play our part and help with jobs around the home—cooking, cleaning, shopping, you know, all of it—but Mum was the manager and organizer for everything to get done and sometimes not done. Growing up on a rural property had its ups and downs, but it made us all resilient and ready for the world ahead when we would one day leave the nest and head out on our own terms with life.

Dad died when I was little. He had an accident at work at the mill. I remember mum being sad for what seemed an eternity, but her faith in God—after she had gotten over being angry with him—had carried her through some tough times with her grief. Most of us kids were too young to realize the impact of dad's death. We missed him, but we were not devastated like Mum. My two older sisters helped Mum take charge. Only eleven and twelve, Susannah and Jeannie jumped on board with Mum to help raise us little ones. I, Sarah, was only five and my little brothers, triplets, were three years old. I loved my sisters. They were like mums to us when Mum couldn't spread all her attention and affection out to everyone when they needed it. We all did the best we could under the circumstances.

Luckily we were part of a good community, so we were helped and taken care of in many ways as we too helped and cared for others in our community. My three little brothers, Lou, Jerry, and Wade, had lots of bigger friends in the church family who would come over after school and play with them, kick a ball around, and take them fishing. We didn't live too far from the coast, half an hour's drive, so the beach was often an exciting and cost-effective way to have some family fun with lots of space to run and play. Often, Mum would invite other friends so she could have some adult company while us kids were having fun.

There were other solo parents in the church, so they all formed a friendship group that often helped each other out with babysitting when someone had to work late, was sick, had an emergency, or anything else life would throw their way.

Not all of us kids in the community grew up on the straight and narrow. Some went wayward…way wayward! Nancy Alcorn was one of those girls. With a dad who liked women too much and a mum who gave up caring, Nancy, an only child, became one of the wildest girls I knew. Drinking, smoking, drugs, and boys—Nancy had a bad reputation and a future that seemed hopeless. No one with any respectability wanted to be seen around her, and no parent wanted their sons or daughters to associate with her. The only respectable adult who would ever go near her was Pastor Lee. Pastor Lee knew what it was like to be ostracised. After years of living on the streets as a teenager and then becoming a pastor in her later years after being born again, she understood wayward kids well. Thank God for Pastor Lee and her understanding and lack of discrimination because years later, Nancy too would come to know God and help save many souls and lives from destruction. In years to come also, she became one of my best friends and one of the greatest women of God I have ever known. Lucky for all of us God doesn't discriminate!

Another girl whose life was also vastly different from mine and Nancy's was Suellen Richards. I didn't actually meet Suellen until I went into training as a missionary at nineteen, but her childhood had its share of challenges as well. Suellen too grew up on a rural farm but was raised by foster parents. After being passed from family to family from an early age, Suellen finally landed with a family who adopted her when she was twelve. She lived in rural outback Australia and ate red dust every day for breakfast, so she would say as we laughed around the campfire in years to come.

Suellen grew up with huge rejection issues. After she was given to a boarding home as a small child and never knowing who her natural parents were, she grew through her childhood feeling lost, alone, and unwanted. When she finally met her foster parents who ended up adopting her as their own when she was twelve, she began to experience the love of family. Suellen's new parents were also a part of a bigger family as well, God's family. The next seven years would bring incredible healing to Suellen's life and set her free from the ashes of rejection. Finally at the age of fifteen, she felt she belonged. The underlying fear that this could all be taken away at any minute, fear that followed her as a child being passed from foster family to foster family, gradually diminished. Secure in love in a spiritual family and knowing that God would never leave her or forsake her, Suellen grew in leaps and bounds.

Over the coming years, Nancy, Suellen, and I developed in our faith. We all had our different unique way of seeing God and the world around us, but the core of our faith in Jesus Christ bound us together in friendship so strong that it felt nothing could shake it. When we all finally met up at Bible college at nineteen and chose the same subjects especially missionary ministry, we had begun a journey that would take us into some of the most challenging and needy situations on the planet. It was time to thrive. It was time to put into practice years of teaching and shaping of our hearts and minds to the will of the Father's destiny for us. His plan had the three of us in a bond so strong that through it, multitudes would be saved and set free from oppressive and dangerous situations.

At twenty-one, we were ready to head out. God was sending us. Africa has had her share of hardships and pain. I was astounded at how much our African brothers and sisters have endured over so many years. On learning about the atrocities that they have faced—apartheid, child soldiers, starvation, genocide, etc.—my heart gave way to the call that God had placed inside my heart to join the ranks of so many missionaries in this country fighting for the freedom of so many in despair. We were sent to Uganda. Child soldiers were rampant in the area. Families with ill and impoverished parents or no parents at all were captured and trained to commit acts of murder, persecution, and a myriad of other atrocities against the innocent for the sake of power and domination.

As we said our good-byes to our families we headed to the plane that would fly us to our destination.

The flight was long and tedious, but we endeavored to keep our good humor, sing songs, and encourage each other. A team of fifty, we were headed to start up a new shelter for children saved from their abductors.

A multitude of skilled people came on board for this mission. We had pastors, doctors, lawyers, medicos, teachers, counselors, cooks, cleaners, and builders. We were trained to be teacher's aides and to help teach the gospel and the love of Christ to these little ones. Our training would continue so we could teach our

African friends to survive and take care of their needs and future generations.

Some of the team were seasoned missionaries, so we were in good hands as far as being led and taught how to operate a missionary station. All were Christians and had his strength.

At 9:50 a.m., we landed at Kenya airport, a major airport that bustled with activity. The atmosphere of Africa filled our senses. Tired and weary, we went through the motions of collecting our baggage and following our leaders onto awaiting buses to take us to a nearby motel where we would rest and restore for a few days before heading out to the mission campsite. Other team members had gone before us to setup camp; they were accompanied by armed soldiers and governing authorities.

Fear could definitely take hold of a heart in this place, but faith and trust in God's goodness overrode it. Being with so many other Christians in a team and the soldiers appointed to guard our camp helped to settle any anxiety that was trying to take hold.

Nancy, Suellen, and I were given our own tent. They were army tents. Tough and dark green, lighting was essential. Solar lights, which need regenerating through the day, were given to each tent. We were responsible for their recharge, and we were also responsible for getting to meals on time, meetings on time, and work situations on time. There was also play time, so it wasn't all grit and grime.

Our first appointed tasks were kitchen duty. We would help prepare vegetables, cook meat, boil rice, and so on, and help with cleanup. We were part of a task force.

The beautiful thing about being part of a Christian missionary task force is that every morning we would wake up and get to worship Jesus with all our other brothers and sisters and then again in the afternoons before the sun would set and before dinner. Each day, we were encouraged from God's word before we commenced so we would carry God's message for us into our day. This created such a beautiful atmosphere, which completely alleviated any fear or anxiety. As we focused our minds on him and the tasks ahead for the day, we were completely occupied with kingdom purposes, God's purposes.

There was much to be done. It was amazing how much would get done in a day with Jesus with us. Our yokes seemed easy and our burdens light, but we managed as a team to achieve so much each day. None of us felt like we were under a yoke of slavery.

As the days and weeks passed, so did any doubts, fears, or reservations about our future in this environment. As little children and big children were being saved and brought to the shelter, it became all about them and not us. They were little broken ones carrying such heavy loads in their souls; some who were forced to kill, rape, torture came with such deep brokenness that only Jesus could repair and set them free.

Many fainted in our arms when we explained to them they were safe now. Our hearts broke time and time again, but we did learn how to manage our emotions so that we wouldn't become emotionally crippled from the extraordinarily sad situations we faced. Tiny children and babies came to us who had been horribly and devastatingly tortured or abused. Their mummies and daddies were tortured and killed; some of their killers being now with us, children soldiers who were saved. I couldn't dwell on the evil that would do such things. I needed to dwell on Jesus and the road of healing and restoration for these little ones. The counselors and pastors were very busy with helping the traumatized and supporting new missionaries, including us, cope with the pain.

As God's love grew in our environment, it felt as if a piece of heaven had landed in this arid place. Over our mission grounds, there seem to be a protective light-and-love-filled bubble that no evil could penetrate. On one occasion in the four months we had now been there, an armed man tried to enter in to take one of our saved boys back into his regime. It turned out to be the boy's uncle. As he tried to enter the grounds, prayer rose up, and the soldiers captured the man. He was brought before governing authorities and questioned about his regime. Eventually he broke down and claimed he too was taken captive into the army as a teenage boy, and they had trained him to lead a platoon.

He had killed and tortured many. As he served his time in jail, he now has hope for his soul as he gave his heart and life to God so it can be turned around for the better. He now ministers to other inmates who have been captured from soldiering who now have a chance of their souls being redeemed.

———◈———

She cried for a long time. Missy, we called her, only about two, had been picked up by one of our scouting teams, armed men on the lookout for child victims or any victims of the regimes. Missy had been placed under a tree to die. She was malnourished, had been beaten and abused, and was incredibly terrorized and traumatized. When they bought her in, we were all shattered. The medico immediately ran to her aid and hooked her up with IVs to rehydrate her and started attending to her wounds. To know that the evil of humanity could come to this bought waves of dread over my soul. I had to take it to God! As I assisted the doctors and nurses, pastors came in to pray and minister over Missy and to comfort her when she awoke. She woke up screaming. The terror that gripped her needed to be soothed so she wouldn't exhaust herself. She was held for a very long time by one of our pastors as the presence and love of God filled the room. Prayer intercessors were behind the scenes, praying for her and her recovery. As God's peace continued to fill the room, she settled into sobs, looking around at everyone, still with terror in her eyes, but gradual settling as she started to sense that she was in a safe environment. The thoughts of her attackers and what was done to her would resurface in her memory time and time again, upsetting her, but soon to be settled by a round-the-clock team member who was there for her. As days passed into weeks, Missy became more trusting and settled. As God was healing her, her memories lessened of the events, and new memories were taking over. Memories of singing, laughing, playing, love, and nourishment. Missy was getting better day by day, soon to be running around with other children, kicking balls, laughing, and clapping her hands in joy. Everyone loved Missy. She was never left alone. There was always someone by her side ministering love to her. She was safe.

Many other children filled our lives with their tragic circumstances and pain, but God had a redemptive plan for these little ones. Plans that would help them recover from the war to their souls. Plans of restoration and healing. Plans of a new life.

As months and then years went by, our mission village grew. I couldn't imagine being anywhere else on the planet other than here, what I was called to do. Nancy, Suellen, and I had become the well-known tight trio. We were, get it done, sisters. No matter what problems were presented at Heaven on Earth (the name given to the mission in earlier days), a solution was not far at hand with us three on top of the problem. The three of us had become the head teachers at the schools and were on the committee for the whole of the mission. God's plan didn't leave us there though. In another two years, we three would be the managers and primary heads of the mission. As we grew into new leadership positions, so too did Heaven on Earth. Schools numbering five thousand children, a hospital to house sick mums and dads of some of our children, and a hospice for those dying of aids and other diseases—Heaven on Earth became a home with stories of thousands being redeemed by God's love.

Ten years on, Nancy, Suellen, and I were running the mission. With God as our head, there were times we needed to pray and fast and seek his wisdom in how to handle different situations. We three were supported by an amazing team of God's servants. Every one of them had a servant's heart for the mission. Selflessness was the gift of everyone on board this great ship. Multitudes of lives were being saved from torture, enslavement, and regimes across this nation. People would travel across the land to find shelter at Heaven on Earth. News had spread throughout this nation of the work God was carrying out through our mission.

Now in our early thirties and leading a very fulfilled and full life for Jesus, little did we know that God had some other plans for us. The three of us saw ourselves on the mission for a long time. With journeys back to Australia to see our families, now being rare opportunities, God was doing some work behind the scenes to reward us three beyond what we could ever have imagined. By the end of the year, I would be married, with my first child underway, Nancy would be sent back to Australia to start a mission in Central Australia, and Suellen would continue work with me, but only for another year before she too would be married and sent back to Australia with her husband, Larry, to start a group housing project for homeless teenagers in Sydney. Everything changes. My husband, Gerard, who I would meet at the mission, an engineer, would continue to help me expand and run the mission for the next twenty years. Both Suellen and Nancy would be raised by God in their new callings to become two of Australia's most recognised humanitarian leaders in the country. Wow!

———◆———

Gerard had landed on our door step, literally, in the summer of 2003. As I opened the door to our home, I saw standing there before me a tall, rugged, unshaved stranger dressed in kaki and wearing an Akubra hat. Gerard was quite a big fellow with a rugged appearance, but before too long, I got to know the gentleness and compassion of this man for the people of Africa. He wasn't a stranger to this land. He had actually done a lot of growing up in Soweto, so he knew oh too well the hardships of this place and what it had done to our African brothers and sisters.

My first glance at Gerard made my heart leap, which indicated he was part of God's plan for my future. At that moment, I didn't realize how deep into that plan our relationship would go.

It was only after about six months of meeting Gerard that near death for us all took place. We had heard of a group of children who were captive, being beaten, and abused by rebel soldiers in the tablelands north of the mission. Scouters who had crossed the border to this region came back to report what was going on. The warfare in that area had escalated and was so fierce that government authorities had retreated their troops as too many were being killed. The rebels had taken over this region and fought violently to keep it that way.

The scouters explained that there was a way to reach the children, but it was very dangerous. We would need to follow a part of the Nile through rugged bushland to reach them, but it could be done.

Gerard immediately started to gather a crew of men, soldiers, to do the journey. I argued with him for a very long time to allow Suellen, Nancy, and me to go with him—I wouldn't allow anyone else from the mission to go; it was too dangerous—as the children would need immediate medical care and attention emotionally. Being women the children would not be as afraid as if it were just the men…they may think that they were just more abusers taking them somewhere else. I knew there could be gunfire and lives lost and possibly our own but these children needed us to help them. God would protect us!

We packed up the truck with supplies, and we, together with ten armed men, headed out. Many bid us farewell. Many prayed.

It was a long dusty drive. Typical scenes of Africa filled our senses. Giraffes foraging for a lunchtime feed, elephants and their young hydrating and playing in muddy waters, cheetahs scooting across the fields at phenomenal rates, and the occasional rhino coming close to our vehicle to check us out. The animals and wildlife were the least of our worries.

One day had passed, and we set up camp along the Nile and rested from a day of searing heat and gusty winds. Fatigue and sunburn had set in, and I was desperate for a cool wash. The Nile is a dangerous place filled with man-eaters, so we filled tubs from the river and moved away from its edges so as not to become a snap surprise for an awaiting crocodile.

I was aware that as I was bathing, I needed protection from anyone or anything that may want to come and attack me in surprise, so Gerard was close by watching out for any signs of danger.

I was uncomfortable though. I had grown very fond of Gerard in the short time we had known each other. He was a good man, with good intentions and a kind heart. I also had references as to his character from many organizations he had been involved with, so I knew this man was a man of integrity. I don't think I would have trusted anyone else to do the job he was doing right now, watching over my safety while being vulnerable. I had erected a small tarp between a tree and a bush for privacy, but my feet and lower legs were still visible as was my shoulders and head above the tarp. The tub was immediately in front of me, so I didn't have to walk far to refresh my sponge.

Gerard started the conversation as the sun was setting and as he roamed the area with sharp eyesight as I safely bathed. "So why a missionary in Africa?" he asked with his white South African accent.

"A dream as a little girl for an extraordinarily adventurous life," I replied.

"Ha," He replied. "You chose that well." We both laughed.

"Actually I believe God chose it for me." Silence.

"How do you know it was God?" he asked.

"Because I've had this dream burning in my heart for a very long time, and each time I prayed if it was his will for me, a scripture on my heart would confirm that this was his will for my life. Life circumstances all took shape to lead me in this direction. I met Nancy and Suellen, who are my dearest friends, and their dream, or our call, as us Christians put it, was the same. I believe God drew the three of us together to be an encouragement and strength to each other along the way."

"Well, that's extraordinary!" We both laughed again.

"So where do you see yourself in ten years' time?"

Without hesitation I replied, "Still here." We smiled at each other. A new warmth touched my soul, and I wondered if it touched his.

Gerard walked me back to camp. After dinner, we sang praises to God around the campfire, and Gerard read a passage from the Bible. We discussed what that passage meant to each of us then went to bed. Gerard and I caught a glance of each other as I retired into my tent, and he stood on guard for his shift. We both smiled. The warmth again.

We were up before daybreak. It was important we weren't seen by poachers or any other enemies. A quick pack-up, and along the way, praise and breakfast had us ready for the journey ahead.

We would be there by nightfall.

We had to leave the vehicle some distance away from where the children were. We hid it in some thick bushlands, disguised it well so that the only way it could be spotted was if you were standing two feet away. The rest of the journey would be done very carefully and on foot. Hiding as we went, camouflaged by clothing that blended with our surrounds, we would be hard to spot from a distance.

As we approached the area where the rebels had set up their headquarters, I could spot a number of small children wandering around. Suddenly two men were talking, and the children were gathered up and shoved into a small hut. I had no idea how many children were in there. Two guards were put on the door. Some time later, a man went into the hut. We just watched the activity until nightfall.

To get to the children, Gerard and one other soldier quietly snuck around the back of the camp through thick foliage, careful not to break and snap any twigs or make sounds that would alarm the rebels. Years of military training for both these men had equipped them for such a time as this.

On reaching the hut, a little girl caught Gerard's eye, and he motioned her to keep quiet. Luckily, she understood. She motioned the other children to keep quiet too—twelve in all—and pointed toward Gerard. One by one, he motioned them to come his way very, very quietly. The two guards were chattering outside the hut, so they were totally unaware as to what was taking place. As all the children were gathered, they began their journey back to us. This time, they needed to enter the waters of the Nile along its banks so as not to make any noise in the foliage. The dark of the night kept them well hidden. We prayed there were no crocodiles.

They made it back safely, but the danger had not ended. Some burst into tears when they reached us; comfort was very needed as was urgent medical care for some. We returned quickly to the truck and loaded everybody in. In the distance, a loud whistle shrilled down the river. An empty hut had been discovered. It was time to run.

The truck flew across the fields at such a dangerous rate, but the danger chasing us was even more threatening. We could see lights in the distance. I thought maybe two or three, but it turned into a six jeeps chasing us. Gunfire.

The children screamed, and we did our best to comfort them and tried to quiet them so the men could focus on our attackers.

We needed to get to the bridge. If we could reach the bridge in time, the men could create a decoy, so we could get away with the children. We did, while crying out to Jesus all the way.

One of the attackers' jeeps had overturned. One down. Thank you, Jesus. Another lost control from a flat tire. Thank you, Jesus. Four were left on hot pursuit, shouting and firing.

The men pulled the truck up at the other side of the bridge when we had crossed blocking the exit.

"Everybody out!" cried Gerard.

He grabbed both my arms, looked me in the eye, and said, "*Run.*"

We couldn't look back. The gunfire was torturous to listen to.

We ran hard.

We ran and ran and ran. Some of the little ones fainted with heat exhaustion. We had no idea where we were running to. We just knew we had to keep moving. The night took us through territory that we had no idea of its hidden dangers. There was no looking back.

The sounds of gunfire faded in the distance until we could hear it no more. We had no idea of the battle's outcome or if…any of our team was still alive. Nausea overcame me.

We finally needed to stop. The children could run no more… for now.

I had no idea where we were. Thankfully neither did our enemy.

We had been running for a long time, carrying children where needed, but our children had a strong determination for life. They had been through too much to quit now. I so admired them!

Our youngest was five, and our oldest, twelve. Taken captive to be trained as rebel soldiers. God had another plan for their precious young lives!

We need to rest and sleep. Everyone was tired and hungry. Luckily, we had three water canisters that Gerard had handed me just before we ran. But it wouldn't last long.

I don't know how long we slept, huddled together under the protective canopies of the forest trees. As I awoke I could hear the running of water so somehow we had travelled downstream along the Nile. I thought we were heading west, but we must have curled back toward the river somewhere along the line. Relief swept over me as I knew that if we followed the river, we would find our way back to the mission. Then nausea hit me. My thoughts on the men we had left behind and… Gerard.

My heart sank. I prayed. Nancy and Suellen had just awoken. They joined me.

One by one, the children stirred. All hungry and thirsty and in need of comfort. We gathered some berries that we knew were safe to eat, and the children gratefully and hungrily devoured them. We had little water, so it needed to be rationed. We needed to get to the river and resupply ASAP.

The children wouldn't go near the banks in case danger lurked there, but I would go while Suellen and Nancy prayed.

We found a spot. It was open with a rock ledge that I could safely walk upon the water's edge...or so I thought. Waiting nearby was a twelve-foot croc that was ravenously hungry. As I started to fill the canisters, I could sense something moving towards me. I turned my head slowly to the right, not wanting to alarm any stalker of my flesh when—*bang!*—a shot was fired from afar, and my attacker was dead. I looked alarmingly around but saw no one. I ran as fast as I could to the women and children. We left... running.

Finally we came to a clearing. I recognized the field as one we had driven through on our way to rescue the children. We had come across it on our second day, so that meant we were still quite some way from the mission. We were all so tired and hungry.

Bang! Another gunshot. We ran for shelter. Then we heard it. The sound of a vehicle. We hid as best we could, but the brush was far more sparse than the forest we had recently come from. We huddled together, afraid and praying.

"You girls want a lift?"

I couldn't believe my ears! Gerard! Joy rose up in my heart and a smile so wide one probably could have fitted an antelope in it. We ran. But this time not in fear and panic but in sheer joy to each other. We embraced for what was seconds but seemed eternity.

Gerard had been tracking us for quite some time. He had kept his distance as he continued to watch for anymore rebels perhaps tracking us. The feud at the bridge had ended in bloodshed and with the rebels leaving the scene and heading south down the Nile. Gerard knew there was another bridge kilometers downstream, and that's what they were heading for to track us down.

The men embarked on the truck with no lives lost but one team member injured—shot in the shoulder—and one rebel man killed. So their numbers were still strong. Gerard came after us as quickly as he could. It was hours before they had tracked us. He had finally found us when we stopped for water.

"Why didn't you let me know it was you who took the shot?" I asked.

"Because if the enemy was close by and I had yelled out, they would have known for sure it was us. But just taking a shot, hopefully they just would have assumed it was poachers," he replied.

"You're so clever." We embraced again.

"But they could be close, so everyone quickly into the truck," he motioned.

We were on our way again. Food supplies in the truck were soon devoured by the children, but we were sure to keep some aside for the rest of the journey. Suellen attended to the soldier's wound, and Nancy and I entertained the children with some games and songs.

Night time soon came. There were no signs of the rebels. Gerard said by now they would have crossed the next bridge, so we were still in danger. He radioed ahead to the mission and let them know everything that was going on and that we had the children in our care. Reinforcements were sent, and the team organized themselves for the arrival of the children and us.

We couldn't stop through the night. We had to keep going. If we stopped the, rebels would gain ground on us, and none of us wanted more bloodshed, particularly any of it being the children.

Gerard and our soldiers knew this land so well that they had no trouble navigating through it during the night hours. Night time gave way to dusk, and we were nearing home. Apparently the reinforcements had overtaken us during the night. We were all asleep except for our driver who had waved and motioned at the convoy who passed us. Whoever was tracking us was now dealing with a team far larger than us. We were safe. Thank you, God!

Everyone rested and ate a very well-prepared evening meal. Eventually, our weariness was overtaking and the shock of the last few days. Suellen, Nancy, and I had decided to call it an early night and started heading toward our cottage. They went on ahead of me as I said goodnight to everyone and congratulated the team for an excellent rescue mission. As I walked down the stairs of the kitchen/dining house, a gentle touch held my shoulder.

"Goodnight," Gerard whispered softly.

"Goodnight," I whispered back. We kissed ever so softly after a harsh and cruel journey.

Our feelings and intention for each other were now sealed. As we grew in love, we married five months later.